Vente Drouot rive gauche, 10-12.1976
6.000 f.

POEMS IN PROSE.

THE ARTIST.

ONE evening there came into his soul the desire to fashion an image of *The Pleasure that abideth for a Moment.* And he went forth into the world to look for bronze. For he could only think in bronze.

But all the bronze of the whole world had disappeared, nor anywhere in the whole world was there any bronze to be found, save only the bronze of the image of *The Sorrow that endureth for Ever.*

Now this image he had himself, and with his own hands, fashioned, and had set it on the tomb of the one thing he had loved in life. On the tomb of the dead thing he had most loved had he set this image of his own fashioning, that it might serve as a sign of the love of man that dieth not, and a symbol of the sorrow of man that endureth for ever. And in the whole world there was no other bronze save the bronze of this image.

And he took the image he had fashioned, and set it in a great furnace, and gave it to the fire.

And out of the bronze of the image of *The Sorrow that endureth for Ever* he fashioned an image of *The Pleasure that abideth for a Moment.*

THE DOER OF GOOD.

It was night-time and He was alone.

And He saw afar-off the walls of a round city and went towards the city.

And when He came near he heard within the city the tread of the feet of joy, and the laughter of the mouth of gladness and the loud noise of many lutes. And He knocked at the gate and certain of the gate-keepers opened to him.

And He beheld a house that was of marble and had fair pillars of marble before it. The pillars were hung with garlands, and within and without there were torches of cedar. And he entered the house.

And when He had passed through the hall of chalcedony and the hall of jasper, and reached the long hall of feasting, He saw lying on a couch of sea-purple one whose hair was crowned with red roses and whose lips were red with wine.

And He went behind him and touched him on the shoulder and said to him, "Why do you live like this?"

And the young man turned round and recognised Him, and made

Fortnightly Review. July 1894 (vois bibliography page 73.

gard such important social problems as those of variation and heredity. While recognising that in the past social evolution in man has been almost entirely the product of extra-group selection and of physical selection acting automatically, they are inclined to believe that increasing sense of social responsibility with regard to parentage, followed, as it is sure to be, at a due distance by regulative legislation, is likely in the future to supplement the automatic action of natural selection by a more rapid process of human selection. They do not understand how the success of theories which inculcate greater social regulation in this respect, place socialism from the biological standpoint at a disadvantage as compared with that individualism, which to-day seems directly to encourage the unlimited breeding of the physically and mentally most degenerate classes in the community, and refuses to impose any test as to physique or intellect on the pauper aliens it allows to enter the social group. The pious wish of Darwin that the superior and not the inferior members of the group should be the parents of the future, is far more likely to be realised in a socialistic than in an individualistic state.

In conclusion, then, if biology is very far from being in a position to lay down the dogma that socialism spells degeneration, it is still quite possible that the socialistic movement will react on biological science as it has already done on economic science. No portion of the material for the study of evolution is nearly as plentiful as that dealing with mankind. We have most wide-reaching statistics as to growth and as to mortality; we have most elaborate measurements of a very great variety of organs in many races of men, and even of men separated by considerable intervals of time. The record is, of course, fragmentary in the extreme, but it is probably far better than can ever be attained for any other form of life. Here, then, we may look for some approximate measurement, if it be but a rough one, of the relative numerical importance of the several factors of natural selection. When these investigations have been carried out, it will be time enough to talk about the antagonism of socialistic theory to biological laws. All the evidence, however, that I individually have been able to gather from a naturally limited examination of anthrometric statistics and anthropological facts, distinctly points to the very small part played by intra-group selection in the case of civilised man. If this be so, then the manufacture of biological bogies for socialists is as idle an occupation as that process of planting economic scarecrows round the field of social reform, by which the Manchester School strove for a time to delay their political bankruptcy.

KARL PEARSON.

answer and said, " But I was a leper once, and you healed me. How else should I live ?"

And He passed out of the house and went again into the street.

And after a little while He saw one whose face and raiment were painted and whose feet were shod with pearls. And behind her came, slowly as a hunter, a young man who wore a cloak of two colours. Now the face of the woman was as the fair face of an idol, and the eyes of the young man were bright with lust.

And He followed swiftly and touched the hand of the young man and said to him, " Why do you look at this woman and in such wise ?"

And the young man turned round and recognised Him and said, " But I was blind once, and you gave me sight. At what else should I look ?"

And He ran forward and touched the painted raiment of the woman and said to her, " Is there no other way in which to walk save the way of sin ?"

And the woman turned round and recognised Him, and laughed and said, " But you forgave me my sins, and the way is a pleasant way."

And He passed out of the city.

And when He had passed out of the city He saw seated by the roadside a young man who was weeping.

And He went towards him and touched the long locks of his hair and said to him, " Why are you weeping ?"

And the young man looked up and recognised Him and made answer, " But I was dead once and you raised me from the dead. What else should I do but weep ?"

THE DISCIPLE.

When Narcissus died the pool of his pleasure changed from a cup of sweet waters into a cup of salt tears, and the Oreads came weeping through the woodland that they might sing to the pool and give it comfort.

And when they saw that the pool had changed from a cup of sweet waters into a cup of salt tears, they loosened the green tresses of their hair and cried to the pool and said, " We do not wonder that you should mourn in this manner for Narcissus, so beautiful was he."

" But was Narcissus beautiful ?" said the pool.

" Who should know that better than you ?" answered the Oreads. " Us did he ever pass by, but you he sought for, and would lie on your banks and look down at you, and in the mirror of your waters he would mirror his own beauty."

And the pool answered, " But I loved Narcissus because, as he lay on my banks and looked down at me, in the mirror of his eyes I saw ever my own beauty mirrored."

The Master.

Now when the darkness came over the earth Joseph of Arimathea, having lighted a torch of pinewood, passed down from the hill into the valley.   For he had business in his own home.

And kneeling on the flint stones of the Valley of Desolation he saw a young man who was naked and weeping.   His hair was the colour of honey, and his body was as a white flower, but he had wounded his body with thorns and on his hair had he set ashes as a crown.

And he who had great possessions said to the young man who was naked and weeping, "I do not wonder that your sorrow is so great, for surely He was a just man."

And the young man answered, "It is not for Him that I am weeping, but for myself.   I too have changed water into wine, and I have healed the leper and given sight to the blind.   I have walked upon the waters, and from the dwellers in the tombs I have cast out devils.   I have fed the hungry in the desert where there was no food, and I have raised the dead from their narrow houses, and at my bidding, and before a great multitude of people, a barren fig-tree withered away.   All things that this man has done I have done also.   And yet they have not crucified me."

The House of Judgment.

And there was silence in the House of Judgment, and the Man came naked before God.

And God opened the Book of the Life of the Man.

And God said to the Man, "Thy life hath been evil, and thou hast shown cruelty to those who were in need of succour, and to those who lacked help thou hast been bitter and hard of heart.   The poor called to thee and thou did'st not hearken, and thine ears were closed to the cry of My afflicted.   The inheritance of the fatherless thou did'st take unto thyself, and thou did'st send the foxes into the vineyard of thy neighbour's field.   Thou did'st take the bread of the children and give it to the dogs to eat, and my lepers who lived in the marshes, and were at peace and praised Me, thou did'st drive forth on to the highways, and on Mine earth out of which I made thee thou did'st spill innocent blood."

And the Man made answer and said, "Even so did I."

And again God opened the Book of the Life of the Man.

And God said to the Man, "Thy life hath been evil, and the Beauty I have shown thou hast sought for, and the Good I have hidden thou did'st pass by. The walls of thy chamber were painted with images, and from the bed of thine abominations thou did'st rise up to the sound of flutes. Thou did'st build seven altars to the sins I have suffered, and did'st eat of the thing that may not be eaten, and the purple of thy raiment was broidered with the three signs of shame. Thine idols were neither of gold nor of silver that endure, but of flesh that dieth. Thou did'st stain their hair with perfumes and put pomegranates in their hands. Thou did'st stain their feet with saffron and spread carpets before them. With antimony thou did'st stain their eyelids and their bodies thou did'st smear with myrrh. Thou did'st bow thyself to the ground before them, and the thrones of thine idols were set in the sun. Thou did'st show to the sun thy shame and to the moon thy madness."

And the Man made answer and said, "Even so did I."

And a third time God opened the Book of the Life of the Man.

And God said to the Man, "Evil hath been thy life, and with evil did'st thou requite good, and with wrongdoing kindness. The hands that fed thee thou did'st wound, and the breasts that gave thee suck thou did'st despise. He who came to thee with water went away thirsting, and the outlawed men who hid thee in their tents at night thou did'st betray before dawn. Thine enemy who spared thee thou did'st snare in an ambush, and the friend who walked with thee thou did'st sell for a price, and to those who brought thee Love thou did'st ever give Lust in thy turn."

And the Man made answer and said, "Even so did I."

And God closed the Book of the Life of the Man, and said, "Surely I will send thee into Hell. Even into Hell will I send thee."

And the Man cried out, "Thou canst not."

And God said to the Man, "Wherefore can I not send thee to Hell, and for what reason?"

"Because in Hell have I always lived," answered the Man.

And there was silence in the House of Judgment.

And after a space God spake, and said to the Man, "Seeing that I may not send thee into Hell, surely I will send thee unto Heaven. Even unto Heaven will I send thee."

And the Man cried out, "Thou canst not."

And God said to the Man, "Wherefore can I not send thee unto Heaven, and for what reason?"

"Because never, and in no place, have I been able to imagine it," answered the Man.

And there was silence in the House of Judgment.

The Teacher of Wisdom.

From his childhood he had been as one filled with the perfect knowledge of God, and even while he was yet but a lad many of the saints, as well as certain holy women who dwelt in the free city of his birth, had been stirred to much wonder by the grave wisdom of his answers.

And when his parents had given him the robe and the ring of manhood he kissed them, and left them and went out into the world, that he might speak to the world about God. For there were at that time many in the world who either knew not God at all, or had but an incomplete knowledge of Him, or worshipped the false gods who dwell in groves and have no care of their worshippers.

And he set his face to the sun and journeyed, walking without sandals, as he had seen the saints walk, and carrying at his girdle a leathern wallet and a little water-bottle of burnt clay.

And as he walked along the highway he was full of the joy that comes from the perfect knowledge of God, and he sang praises unto God without ceasing; and after a time he reached a strange land in which there were many cities.

And he passed through eleven cities. And some of these cities were in valleys, and others were by the banks of great rivers, and others were set on hills. And in each city he found a disciple who loved him and followed him, and a great multitude also of people followed him from each city, and the knowledge of God spread in the whole land, and many of the rulers were converted, and the priests of the temples in which there were idols found that half of their gain was gone, and when they beat upon their drums at noon none, or but a few, came with peacocks and with offerings of flesh as had been the custom of the land before his coming.

Yet the more the people followed him, and the greater the number of his disciples, the greater became his sorrow. And he knew not why his sorrow was so great. For he spake ever about God, and out of the fulness of that perfect knowledge of God which God had himself given to him.

And one evening he passed out of the eleventh city, which was a city of Armenia, and his disciples and a great crowd of people followed after him; and he went up on to a mountain and sat down on a rock that was on the mountain, and his disciples stood round him, and the multitude knelt in the valley.

And he bowed his head on his hands and wept, and said to his Soul, "Why is it that I am full of sorrow and fear, and that each of my disciples is as an enemy that walks in the noonday?"

And his Soul answered him and said, "God filled thee with the perfect knowledge of Himself, and thou hast given this knowledge away to others. The pearl of great price thou hast divided, and the vesture without seam thou hast parted asunder. He who giveth away wisdom robbeth himself. He is as one who giveth his treasure to a robber. Is not God wiser than thou art? Who art thou to give away the secret that God hath told thee? I was rich once, and thou hast made me poor. Once I saw God, and now thou hast hidden Him from me."

And he wept again, for he knew that his Soul spake truth to him, and that he had given to others the perfect knowledge of God, and that he was as one clinging to the skirts of God, and that his faith was leaving him by reason of the number of those who believed in him.

And he said to himself, "I will talk no more about God. He who giveth away wisdom robbeth himself."

And after the space of some hours his disciples came near him and bowed themselves to the ground and said, "Master, talk to us about God, for thou hast the perfect knowledge of God, and no man save thee hath this knowledge."

And he answered them and said, "I will talk to you about all other things that are in heaven and on earth, but about God I will not talk to you. Neither now, nor at any time, will I talk to you about God."

And they were wroth with him and said to him, "Thou hast led us into the desert that we might hearken to thee. Wilt thou send us away hungry, and the great multitude that thou hast made to follow thee?"

And he answered them and said, "I will not talk to you about God."

And the multitude murmured against him and said to him, "Thou hast led us into the desert, and hast given us no food to eat. Talk to us about God and it will suffice us."

But he answered them not a word. For he knew that if he spake to them about God he would give away his treasure.

And his disciples went away sadly, and the multitude of people returned to their own homes. And many died on the way.

And when he was alone he rose up and set his face to the moon, and journeyed for seven moons, speaking to no man nor making any answer. And when the seventh moon had waned he reached that desert which is the desert of the Great River. And having found a cavern in which a Centaur had once dwelt, he took it for his place of dwelling, and made himself a mat of reeds on which to lie, and became a hermit. And every hour the Hermit praised God that He had suffered him to keep some knowledge of Him and of His wonderful greatness.

Now, one evening, as the Hermit was seated before the cavern in which he had made his place of dwelling, he beheld a young man of evil and beautiful face who passed by in mean apparel and with empty hands. Every evening with empty hands the young man passed by, and every morning he returned with his hands full of purple and pearls. For he was a Robber and robbed the caravans of the merchants.

And the Hermit looked at him and pitied him. But he spake not a word. For he knew that he who speaks a word loses his faith.

And one morning, as the young man returned with his hands full of purple and pearls, he stopped and frowned and stamped his foot upon the sand, and said to the Hermit: "Why do you look at me ever in this manner as I pass by? What is it that I see in your eyes? For no man has looked at me before in this manner. And the thing is a thorn and a trouble to me."

And the Hermit answered him and said, "What you see in my eyes is pity. Pity is what looks out at you from my eyes."

And the young man laughed with scorn, and cried to the Hermit in a bitter voice, and said to him, "I have purple and pearls in my hands, and you have but a mat of reeds on which to lie. What pity should you have for me? And for what reason have you this pity?"

"I have pity for you," said the Hermit, "because you have no knowledge of God."

"Is this knowledge of God a precious thing?" asked the young man, and he came close to the mouth of the cavern.

"It is more precious than all the purple and the pearls of the world," answered the Hermit.

"And have you got it?" said the young Robber, and he came closer still.

"Once, indeed," answered the Hermit, "I possessed the perfect knowledge of God. But in my foolishness I parted with it, and divided it amongst others. Yet even now is such knowledge as remains to me more precious than purple or pearls."

And when the young Robber heard this he threw away the purple and the pearls that he was bearing in his hands, and drawing a sharp sword of curved steel he said to the Hermit, "Give me, forthwith, this knowledge of God that you possess, or I will surely slay you. Wherefore should I not slay him who has a treasure greater than my treasure?"

And the Hermit spread out his arms and said, "Were it not better for me to go unto the outermost courts of God and praise Him, than to live in the world and have no knowledge of Him? Slay me if that be your desire. But I will not give away my knowledge of God."

A LESSON FROM THE *CHICAGO*.

NELSON once saw an American squadron in European waters. Whether it was Captain Richard Dale's squadron, in 1801, Captain Richard Valentine Morris's squadron in 1802—3, or Captain Edward Preble's squadron in 1803, I do not know; but it is said that the great chief paid much attention to the vessels, and that his verdict was: "There is in the handling of those transatlantic ships a nucleus of trouble for the navy of Great Britain."

The trouble came in 1812. Great Britain had waged for many years a naval war of unexampled proportions, and by devotion and valour had broken the back of the most vigorous maritime combination that, in all her history, had been arrayed against her. The fleets of France, Spain, the Netherlands, and Denmark had, once or oftener, together or singly, been met and beaten as fleets had never been beaten before, and although hostilities still dragged on, Great Britain was entitled, if ever in her career, to consider herself supreme mistress of the ocean. But from the remote West, where Nelson had detected the premonitory warning, an innocent-looking cloud quickly overspread the horizon, and in a short space grew so black and threatening, as to make it appear to many capable observers, that the colossal power which had been built up with so much labour, time, and treasure at the cost of the Old World, was destined to be suddenly, and even easily, shattered by the prentice lightnings of the New.

From the day of the declaration of war by the United States in June, 1812, up to June, 1813, the history of the maritime affairs of Great Britain was, so far as American efforts influenced it, one of almost unrelieved disaster. Quotations from *The Times* of the period will serve to show how the gloom deepened. On October 7th, 1812, that journal said:—

"The loss of a single frigate by us, when we consider how all other nations of the world have been dealt by, ... is but a small one."

On December 26th, 1812, it said:—

"Certainly there was a time when it would not have been believed that the American navy could have appeared upon the sea after a six months' war with England; much less that it could, within that period, have been twice victorious. *Sed tempora mutantur.*"

On December 28th, 1812, it exclaimed, concerning the excuses for the loss of the *Macedonian* :—

"O miserable advocates! Why, this renders the charge of mismanagement far heavier than before! In the name of God, what was done with this

And the young Robber knelt down and besought him, but the Hermit would not talk to him about God, nor give him his Treasure, and the young Robber rose up and said to the Hermit, " Be it as you will. As for myself, I will go to the City of the Seven Sins, that is but three days' journey from this place, and for my purple they will give me pleasure, and for my pearls they will sell me joy." And he took up the purple and the pearls and went swiftly away.

And the Hermit cried out and followed him and besought him. For the space of three days he followed the young Robber on the road and entreated him to return, nor to enter into the City of the Seven Sins.

And ever and anon the young Robber looked back at the Hermit and called to him, and said, " Will you give me this knowledge of God which is more precious than purple and pearls ? If you will give me that, I will not enter the city."

And ever did the Hermit answer, " All things that I have I will give thee, save that one thing only. For that thing it is not lawful for me to give away."

And in the twilight of the third day they came nigh to the great scarlet gates of the City of the Seven Sins. And from the city there came the sound of much laughter.

And the young Robber laughed in answer, and sought to knock at the gate. And as he did so the Hermit ran forward and caught him by the skirts of his raiment, and said to him : " Stretch forth your hands, and set your arms around my neck, and put your ear close to my lips, and I will give you what remains to me of the knowledge of God." And the young Robber stopped.

And when the Hermit had given away his knowledge of God, he fell upon the ground and wept, and a great darkness hid from him the city and the young Robber, so that he saw them no more.

And as he lay there weeping he was ware of One who was standing beside him ; and He who was standing beside him had feet of brass and hair like fine wool. And He raised the Hermit up, and said to him : " Before this time thou had'st the perfect knowledge of God. Now thou shalt have the perfect love of God. Wherefore art thou weeping ?" And He kissed him.

OSCAR WILDE.

www.ingramcontent.com/pod-product-compliance
Ingram Content Group UK Ltd.
Pitfield, Milton Keynes, MK11 3LW, UK
UKHW020128100726
13658UKWH00005B/2419